HER Epicenter

Even Adam Has Secrets

So let me get this right...
Stop my story any time if I'm missing facts
This thing we have or had
Whichever or however you chose it
Was broken due to unforeseen circumstances
It's been delicately brought to my attention
Perhaps all your intentions weren't for the benefit of me but those
we won't mention
Now you see...
You had me well before I knew I wanted you
But you knew that already didn't you?
Let me say some things you didn't know
I know how your smile wraps up
And cause an indent in your brow
I know how when you're upset
Sad, angry and irritated
I know you better than you know you
I know when you lie and omit a truth
I can see into your soul all the things you hide
But you knew that already didn't you?
Just like you knew when I fell in love with you
And that scared you, didn't it?
Because you loved me too
And I use all these past tenses because...

You threw me away like garbage
Disposed of me and called it "healthy"
Then in you swoop with promises of...
The friendship that we started with

All the while knowing my heart was breaking
Then when I think the melted iceberg can reform
You tell me you're fucking her
You have spun me for a loop
You dismissed me to fuck her
To lay between her thighs the way you did mine
And not only did you lie about the time table
You spoke of it as if I wouldn't be hurt
And the more I heard the more I pretended
Pretended to enjoy hearing how someone else
Filled your time
How someone else became your Valentine
And I pasted on a smile and copy and pasted good vibes
All the while it's killing me been killing me
But I saw my opening and I asked
Choose me...fuck her choose me
The answer was simple
It seemed like laughter whispering off your tongue
But you weren't laughing
And on that day I broke a little more
Cause you loved her, you love her

She's beautiful and perfect in more ways I can name
She fits a mold that I didn't know you needed
Didn't know you wanted
And I've seen how you look at her
The way you used to look at me
The glow in your eyes and a skip in your step
That used to belong to me
You used to belong to me in every sense of the word
And this ratchet, smart and beautiful woman took you from me
You turned your back on me
And for something that lasted less than three months
I invested my all in you
And I still do...
Making you into something no one ever could
My words, shit any words for that matter
Make someone into a permanent fixture
Gravitating through this thing we call life
And you do not even know why I do it
You don't know why I dedicate so much to you
Why the fuck do I do that?

Why every time do I come back?
You're something that's stuck to me
Stuck somehow in the depths of me
In my soul maybe...

But I hate you
I hate that you don't want me
I hate that you can't stand to touch me
I hate that you don't want to see me
I hate that you don't want to build with me
I hate that you lie when you're lying with her
I hate that I have no chance
And most of all I hate myself
I hate myself for loving and being unloved
I hate this friendship we have
That leaves me empty inside
I hate that every time I want to release you
I come right back in hopes
Things might change
But the only constant there is
Is you're still fucking her
And you don't want me
But I'm still waiting around on the maybe
The one that'll never come

And I'm melting into nothing
Because it's nothing I can get right
Stop my story any time if I'm missing facts
This thing we have or had
Whichever or however you chose it
Was broken due to unforeseen circumstances
It's been delicately brought to my attention
Perhaps all your intentions weren't for the benefit of me but those
we won't mention
Now you see...
You always held the key

A Cross Between

What in the absolute fuck?
What is that I smell?
What is that sensation?
It's the cross between...
Here and there
And damn if I can't or can say...
Smells like sweet nectar
The bark on a willow tree
The dew of a hundred roses
And what's that?
It's crisp like...

Like the sea
Is it he? Is it she?
Feeling so soft like the ocean breeze
And I touched her while she slept
Damn...
I couldn't breathe in that instant
My legs frozen in place
My heart thunderous like a drum
Can she hear it?
I don't want to move for fear she wakes
Damn I can't say if she can or can't hear it

I want to stand still
Believe me I fucking do
But I want to fucking do things to you
More like I want to be fucking you
Til the sweet scent of the water that is you
Drips down my chin
Crash into me again...swallow me
Drown me in...in your wave

She is you, you are he
Your skin feels like moss
Your head glistening in the moonlight
Reminding me that you draw to my sun sign
And that ocean that overflowed
Now spills between my thighs
And there you are...

Right there claiming me with your spirit
Placing your roots into my earth
And when did we become flesh
When did this happen?

What in the absolute fuck?
What is that I smell?
What is that sensation?
It's the cross between...
Here and there
And damn if I can't or can say...
Smells like sweet nectar
The bark on a willow tree
The dew of a hundred roses
And what's that?
It's crisp like...

The smell of the sea

Not Your Average Eve

Fuck you, yeah I'm on that fuck you shit
I tried to lie to you, rather lie with you
And here you go with your lying ass
Twisting my words into corkscrew tales
Who do you think I am?
Who was there to pick up the fucking pieces?
Nigga that was me
Feeding hope into your ears
Letting you know the kingship that runs in your veins
That was me, you fucking dummy
Those pieces that you didn't even know were broken
I helped glue you back together
And you treat me like I'm some off the block
Concrete; rose growing out the weeds
Type bitch...

I'm not sure where you got fucking confused
Maybe it was when you had too much to drink
Having the hangover from hell
Leaving your brain without a memory
Of who the fuck I am
I birthed the language you fed your wife
And fucked the shit out of you
While you whispered them to her
Shit...you don't remember?
Then we play this friendship game
Where I'm being perfect Penny
And all sunshine and fucking rainbows
And who are you?
Leaving simple sentences in my inbox
We are friends right my nigga?
Thick as thieves right my nigga?
I'm finding you the epitome of a stereotype
When a nigga can't contemplate verbal stimulation he turns into
nothing more than a fly on the wall
 Shaking my head
And I'm wasting my fucking efforts writing you into existence
Shit writing you into an everlasting being
I just made your ass into an immortal
Again I've placed you first
But least I know how to say...
Fuck you, yeah I'm on that fuck you shit

Tube Television

I see you in technicolor
Brilliant colors splashed across the screen

Your motions clambering across the pavement
There's something filthy about you
I'm not sure if it's...
in the streetlight you call your soul
Or in the blackened night that you've named your vision
When did your merriment become a sickness

And I'm so angry at myself
For falling for these black and white pictures
Filled with lifeless eyes and a body
A body known for passion and desensitized
Where do they create you?
What horrors have your mind digested?
Do you think there's something filthy about you?

Reborn

I blacked out in your eyes
I don't know when it happened
In fact...I'm sure it was the first time...
The first time I heard your voice
So clearly responding to my name
Your voice stroked me
In places long since sleep

That's where our story began...

I littered your phone with my wit
You embraced my words
As if they were...a disease
Not in the typical sense
In the sense where they spread across you
And leave in their wake something...
Something both damaging and intriguing

Our story grew...

Something about secret messages
Eating away the daylight
Whispered innuendos clinging to the night
I thought I found solace with you
A thing I thought I would never find again

Our story became stagnant...

You are of my walls with your poetry
You dove into me relentlessly
Because I named to you all the ways
I needed, wanted gravitated towards

Being possessed...
Yes possessed...
To allow you to become an imprint on my skin
Loving me roughly and stroking me with hopes

Ever finding, ever ending story...

You made love to my mind
Melded with me the way no other has
And you robbed me of words
To describe the hold you have on me
So I try to write it in simple poetry
Hoping that my symmetry will somehow
Justify the need that has become a hunger
Within the pit of my stomach
"Experience" you call it
This situation ship we have

A story...

While I think of what you do to me
Doing to her and whomever else
I realize it's not you, it's me
Asking more of you
And being blinded by the offering you gave
The sweet hopelessness you plagued me with
Reminding me of what it feels like to be held
To be cherished in this moment
The world stops spinning
And I feel safe until I realize
My time and your time is not "our time"
And I am wandering down the rabbit hole
Holding onto the fact that one day
Someday soon you could love me
Maybe?
And then I realize this "experience"
Is just an experiment
For you to pretend with me
Until you're able to pretend with someone else

I'm not sure when this story started making me feel...
Feel in love...feel cherished...feel something

But you know what?
This whatever this is...isn't growing
It's not budding into anything
Because all of this was a lie
And it's my fault for lying with you
Divulging my secrets to you
Like pen to paper and allowing you in
King to my Queen you were not
The Nile split us long before you entered
My temple; lusting for my flesh
You give no love, so it's my fault I fell

No fairy tale story...

I loved it while I was in it
And I hate it that I need it
All I want is you...
Now there's nothing more to do
You're not capable of love

Goddess Awakened

One day I woke up and saw humanity in my eyes
I saw all the hues...
I remember when I carried your heart in my pocket
I remember when I dusted the helplessness from your eyes
The doubt from your hands and the sadness in your walk
I remember when I breathed inspiration into your lungs
Don't you remember?

Of course you wouldn't...
The drive that sits on your soul
The madness that has taken your mind
You've forgotten of whence you came
The glimmer of hope you claim in your eyes
Is nothing more than spray painted contentment
Maybe you resent me...
Because sometimes your memory
Brings back things I did that taunt you
Humiliate you even

But I saw the rainbow in your footprints
That never ending beauty that I couldn't look away from
That perfection right after the storm
You can't feel what you are worth?
You can't fathom what you were made to do
Let me show you who you are

Hold my hand for this journey...
Close your eyes and let me show you

There, just beyond the clearing
The lush green leaves and hand like branches
This thicket here...covered in hibiscus
You were born here
Pollinated in this flower
You were so sweet budding
Into this death defying King
You held the forest in the palm of your hand
I allowed you command over the domain
At least pre maturely...it was mine after all
I welded you into a great warrior
Made you a vision and poured the night sky into you
I filled you with clouds, sun, moon and stars
And I still had work to do

You don't remember your awakening
You don't remember who you are
You came from greatness
Earth shattering, mind controlling, awe inspiring
Greatness...

My love you are my greatest creation
Blood of my blood
Heart of my heart...
You are my greatest weapon and mine to weld

One day I woke up and saw humanity in my eyes
I saw all the hues...
I remember when I carried your heart in my pocket
I remember when I dusted the helplessness from your eyes
The doubt from your hands and the sadness in your walk
I remember when I breathed inspiration into your lungs
Don't you remember?
Don't you remember your Creator

Moonshine

Experiences...
Blessed like honey between these thighs
I sometimes prey for you
Or pray on you...
You won't see what I did there
Before I've done what you see here

They say you need to chase me with a lime
As if the sweet, salty and tangy taste of me
Needs to be tampered...temper tempered
Is what the issue is...as if I'm glass
But no breakthrough on these sweet pieces of nectar

You called out to me little bee
Pollinating all the lovely flowers around me
Leaving your scent on the air
And I sent for you as all good Queens do
And then in that moment you struck
Like a star me from the sky and I died
So many quick deaths I can't fathom breathing
But don't weep for me

These deaths didn't involve any resuscitation
Unless when it comes to mouth to mouth

You mean your lips on my lips
The lips found at my hips
Dancing and doing what womb walkers do

Conjuring your looks
Lusting for your touch
All the while you're still lost
Wondering how you love my body this much
I could tell you of all the times we have done this
Century after century...but for now that just isn't in me

Queen of the Days

They named me Queen

Long before I even understood

Understood the meaning

Or what it meant for me

What legacy lay within my veins

What royalty laced my blood

They named me Queen

Long before I knew what was in a name

Long before I knew what I was

Long before I distinguished myself as "she"

Long before the womb identified me

They named me Queen

For the passing of breath

For the thoughts of the Nile

For the healing whip marks of the slaves

For the length of this continent

They named me Queen

Filled the molding of this making

Into a clay predestined to be

More than I could be

More than I should be

All that I can be

They named me Queen

They say they named me it for the Ocean

They say the Ocean was made for me

Or did they say me for it

They say I was born and it grew vast

Is that who named me?

The waters?

They say I was born of her

Born to embrace what she brings

Life they told me...

They said she molded me from clay

She covered me in algae

And smothered me with molten rock

To forge a heartbeat into me

They said

To make my skin warm

To make my breath hot

And to make my skin the color...

The color of ash...

Ash? No...the color of the land

They said I was made for the land

They say they named me Queen

They named me Queen for as I took my first steps

The ground shook below me

The earth opened up and plants started to grow

They said my first steps brought life to land

They call me Queen before I was able to stand

Stand on my own two feet

Before I was able to babble

Suck my thumb

Or nurse

My heart pounding in my ears

Life blood making changes to the land

They called me Queen

Long before I even understood

Understood the meaning

Understood the syllables

Understood the weight of it

My footsteps pound the concrete

Breaking bread with addiction

Thriving off of premature existence

Pedaling happiness disguised as love

I've come here to change your definition

Of me...of she...of her...of us...of we

This crown we carry

This burden we bury

To make and renew life

Not just in the present but in the future

In the past tense of you

All the yous

Until you recognize what I've known all along

I birthed the Nile

I gave breath to every village ten-fold

I ran my fingers along the spine of Israel

And made temples in my name

I held the neck of Giza

And bred her children

I split my soul in half and threw it into the Ocean

And there you see that's where your madness came from

The West...you've forgotten me

I made you what you are

You eat of my land

Stumble on my streets

Poison my waters and yet here I stand

Accepting of you

Littering you with children

Giving you the ability to choose

Remember these gifts

As you remember my name

I am and forever will be

The Great I Am

Elohim

Messiah

Mary

Jacob

Job

Ebrahim

But you...you can call me Queen

Now...bow

Excuse me, Black Girl

Excuse me Black Girl, is there a reason why lies lie in your eyes before you allow them to escape your mouth? Is it the fact that there's so much pain hidden in the sentences you rather melon drop coat it? Black Girl don't you know I can see who you are?

I know the pain and desperation you have gone through and I know you allowed yourself to be dependent on their emotions to find your happy...we all have to do that sometimes

Black Girl, I hear the secrets that you whisper into the night. It seems you have no diary invested in others just into this darkness where you were lost at to begin with...you find solace in its silence?

Black Girl the manipulation bleeds off you like tears on a stained baby's face. Why conjure disillusioned shots on your life? Allowing others to be blanketed in the nonsense built on the pretense of you still being in existence by receiving attention.

Black Girl I see you shy away from your own shadow...the night is what scares you more than all the days combined. No was never an answer you used or use clearly but now I hear it ringing from your lips.

The same lips that swore they didn't want me...the same lips that

swore they were through...the same lips that kissed me good night...

Black Girl...I know you may be afraid but the woman I mind fucked

is in there too...

Give her time to breathe...

Then Black woman come home where you belong

Bittersweet

When the justification rose from my mouth like violence

 I knew right then there would be no turning back...

There would be no alternate ending as I watch you disappear from

sight

Mirrors are not the only things that cause illusions

I drank from the cup

I drank from the cup

RE-generated

Wait you told me to act like I'm better
You told me to plagiarize what it means to be me
By dictating my life down onto empty pages
Writing fantasies into folk lore
Hoping that the present tense of the words will overflow
Will make my life then over pour with what...
The emotion unbeknownst to me
They say you can catch it in the water
Maybe I was poisoned by the pond
I feel things bubbling up in me like a volcano
Wait...wait...
Don't bombard me...
I'm out here acting better
To be better and keep distance between half-filled glasses
Ones that aren't aware that my pouring
Is to special and that there is no room for me to spill
I won't continue to fill half-filled glasses and leave mine
All but empty
Today is the first step
In realizing and always remembering
To...wait...
And know that it'll happen

Roleplay Both Ways

I want your box wide open for me
I want to see all of you
Spread before me
As my entree and dessert
I want to feast upon you
Like you've never been eaten before
And I'm not talking about the nectar
Between your thighs
I speak of the mental box
The one that your brain is encased in
I want to open every flap
Ever so gently
Cause I know it's hard on you
I know the pain you've been through
So slowly I'll penetrate you
Take your mind on a ride
And hold you in those times

I want you open for me
The way trees love bees
The way fall loves leaves
The way Greeks loved Hercules

Strip down bare before me
I know it's hard...
I can see the battle in your eyes
I am not here to hurt you
I am here to show you
How good it feels
To release the chains of your mind

To fall into the trap that time
Has taken and know...
I'll catch you

Our friendship has just blossomed
Yet it doesn't feel new
If you asked me to I would do it
Anything for you
Simply because you are you
You've touched something deep in me
Something that burns and cools
All at once...
Fire and ice they call it
I wish to ignite

But...

I want you open for me
The way trees love bees
The way fall loves leaves
The way Greeks loved Hercules

Silly as it may sound...for you I will be
Anything more and everything else
I'll grant you any wish
My hands can make true.
My dear...there's no one like you

Prelude

Now listen...
The curve of your smile
Causes my lips to quiver
In a want that was unexplainable
The way you laid your hand against my thigh

Possession they call it...
At that moment I was yours
Yours to claim
And all you had to do was ask...
I felt the nectar of your kiss
On my glass
I wanted to sip it slow
So the imagery of my lips against yours
Was something I could treasure
I grasped the neck of it...
As if holding your chin
And the mouth of the glass
Your stained lips
You sip that beer
Like a woman thirsting on something
Perhaps your spirit is lost
Something like that lemon
You push into the bottle
Is that it?
Are you lost little bird?
I see your wings trying to spread
As you glimpse in my direction
You take a sip
And excuse yourself for a smoke
Are you running?
Is the temperature here burning you
As it does me...
Your possession left behind your warmth
I still felt your hand in your absence
What do they call this?
A crush

Woman Crush Wednesday

She makes me wanna be better
Be the sun in her smile
She make me wanna be greater
Be the dip in her hip when she walks
She makes me wanna be driven
Be the thoughts inside her mind
She makes me wanna live better
Be the wind that carries her forward
She makes me wanna cry longer
At the thought of never making love to her
She makes me wanna dig deeper
And crush my soul into hers
She makes me want to stay hungry
And eat her words like sweet nectar
She makes me want to beg for it
Be her wall when she gets weak
She makes me want to give more
Be the laughter everyone seeks
She makes me want to enjoy the run
Be the stride she's forgotten to walk
She makes me want...
Her like I've never wanted another woman
Like a breath of fresh air
She makes me want...
To flow into her river
Crash into her waves
Drown in her spirit
And gasp for breath
She makes me want to cum at the sound of her voice
She makes me want to tease myself just a bit more
Beg my mind to conjure more words
To how much I could adore her
Mainly...
She makes me humble
Because there's no greater gift then she could give me...

Besides herself
She is my Queen

Sensitive Flesh

Let me be your safe place...come place your body in front of mine in this warm water...
I've lit the room and you are the star...I'm trying so hard to focus on just washing your smooth skin. I smell the side of your neck and you smell like a treat from my childhood...I can't help but lick a line from your collar bone to the tip of your ear...my hands are hungry...massaging, caressing, pinching...until I've found your breast. So sensitive to the touch...pinching...my eyes watching your labored breathing...fuck...I can see your lips peeking at me through the water...I leave one hand pinching your nipple. The other hand massaging down belly, your hip, skip to your thigh...spreading your legs open...my breath catches...and I hold my breath and then I rub my fingers down your clit. Oh God...you feel amazing and I'm shaking with the want of you...I'm trying to focus...and my fingers have a mind of their own...I feel you melting against me...I'm massaging your clit...just that tip right there...you know the one...the one that makes your eyes cross...I feel the dew moving over my fingers even in the water. I know my fingers can drive you to the peak...but I want you to crash...
I move my hands away...rinse the soap off your skin...wrap you in a towel, bring a candle and lay you on the bed...I crawl up from the bottom of the bed spread your legs wide...
Kiss your feet from the instep all the way up your thighs...kneading and kissing...I blow on your clit...your back arches...I move up your

body. Nibble your waist, lick your nipples, make my mark on your
neck and lick the seams of your lips and kiss you til your
breathless...and on the intake of your breath push fingers into
honey. Fuck woman...and I can't kiss you anymore...
I claim your clit with my lips...ride my tongue...hold me here...cum
for me...show me where it feels good...break...and I'm cumming just
thinking of you cumming in my mouth...
God...you must taste like Heaven

First Came the Rib

Was it Monday night or Wednesday night when you called
I can't remember when
Of all the grins I wish to see again
Was it Friday night

When you asked to come between the lights
The sun kisses of my curtains
Was that the night...no...

It must've been one of these weekdays
Where drastically missed glazed eyes
Found themselves at the tips of my fingers
Was that when you thought my bed...
You're in between time...your Hotel California
Where you get to check out but I'm stuck in euphoria

And I've missed this sort of high
Where the delight is not in the pleasure it causes in my veins
The delight is the pain I know I will feel afterwards
The fatality I know better than I know the names of every hour and
minute
The love I have for you is one I know every waking day my dear

I used to imprint on the first man that paid me my due diligence
Garner from him all the things I wished I had
And imbed in him all the things he was missing
As a baby bird does its mother...
I started to cripple these men specifically you
Crippled you into thinking that my desire for temporary insanity
through the melding of bodies would maintain my thirst for you
Honey that's where you lost me

You...you see I met many of yous within the past 10 years of my life
Shit in the last 5 years of my life
And I recall that every single time
I fell for the pain this would cause me over the happy that I could
gain

How much of this energy could I misplace elsewhere
Into my poetry...into drugging myself with knowledge...into bleeding
for humanity...into living for humanity...into loving for it
Instead of me leaving you on read
Hoping your balls stay on blue
But knowing the love I carry inside of me
Would be a waste if I spent that shit on you

I need a dick that can do more then give me just another "one of those nights"; mixed with an empty bed and promises in "the morning". These notches in my bed posts don't amount to much not even a trophy but they give me peeks of what I accept and I listen to the thoughts of my soul in these "echoes of silence" Have you ever been adorned with jewels? Presents for a reminder of something they all seem to call love in this world but yet I think it's forgotten on you and all you know is these "wicked games" You write as if "echoes of silence" plague your soul and you're not sure how to escape so you make it a pretense to distance yourself...I was taught that that is called "the knowing" you stated that asking for attention seemed to be something that made my insecurities shine through. I say let them shine because the light within me is the "cure" and not a "false alarm" I'm not sure when humanity became so biased and disguised in the questions that it's not okay to want to feel or be wanted...as if it is some disease that is an overlay on the skin. If anything, these tender moments are a kind "reminder" that your most animalistic instincts sit right on the surface. Some get lost in the fact that blinking and breathing and forgotten sexual escapades are what blossom life. This "privilege" of life that flutters in our chest conjures us for so much more. I refuse to suffer a "a lonely night" or more "wasted time" waiting on you to decide if you'd like to acknowledge my existence as a woman with more than a heartbeat between my thighs. This sexual violence though an interesting interpretive dance allows me the time to cleanse myself of the pain you may or may not have left in the crevice of my mind and my right ventricle. Now I know better and I am embracing myself the new her I have become..." love through her" is the title of my new story.

Innuendos

Listen to me...

I know what's inappropriate...
Asking you over after a first meeting
The first "hello" the first "goodbye"
After the first hand hold
I know it's not appropriate

I'm getting used to being inappropriate
I'm getting used to printing the thoughts
The feelings...the dripping of this wetness down
I've been imprinting on pages
To cool the beast inside me

The one that rages and rattles in the cage

She saw...rather I saw your lips
And then I felt them...
Right on the pulse of my neck
Felt the lick of your tongue on my collar bone
Felt your strong hands kneading my waist
Fuck...I'm feeling it again

I feel encased here trying to be appropriate
Trying to hide the fact that my lips want your lips
Hide the fact that I have an insatiable appetite
Hide the fact that my mind and body call to yours
What is happening?

I feel you in the very core of me
How is that possible
How can I feel you there?
In a place that I thought was hollowed out
Your spirit calls to mine
What'd you put in that lemonade
To make me catch my breath
Hang on your every word

In those moments in the eyes of the public
If you would've told me to spread my legs
I would have...
If you would have rubbed your hand right
Against the seam where...
You know the spot
I would have let you
I need to feed...I know it and you feel it
I need to run...I need to go

It's after 8...then 9...then 10
And the physical me is begging you to come
To pay worship to my body
To strip these leggings down
Sweatshirt...tee shirt...bare below you
Fuck...I feel it...
And it feels so good, don't you think?

But is it appropriate?

Feverish

His lips look like my last breath
Something so necessary I can't take my eyes off
I've been trying to stare you in your eyes
Focus on your words and this conversation
My eyes keep lingering back to that corner
The corner of your mouth that curves up
When I say something subtle...

That smile disappears as quickly as it came
But I can't stop it
I daydream of the pinkness of them
The specks of red meshed with a little brown
I can feel them on mine...

And as we talk your lips push the envelope
The envelope that lays between my thighs
My breath catches and I re engage
In this conversation over rum and coke
Sitting on barstools...mind fucking you

Went to taste though rum scorched lips
A tango of your tongue tasting of coke
Just place your hand on my back as we leave
You've burned yourself to my mind

And my body knows yours before you touched me
What is this? I want a taste of it
What do you taste like

King Maker

They call me the King maker
I opened up the earth and set them forth
To do with it as they wished
It was my WILL they set out to do
Claiming their inheritance

Their skin ranging from marble to ash
Each of their identities spawned from something...
Some thought...some action...some emotional connection that rages inside me
Some of these irrational manifestations
Spout from my head as if a movie on a screen
And then I sit and I've molded another

Another grave digger, another shape shifter another nation layer

Novelty

When eyes set on foreign skies it appears as if the sun opens up
To burn brighter is an avenue of approach that we don't find often
We cloak peace as radical equality
We garner trust as feverish battles

All the while we could be falling together instead of apart

Have you felt the rise in my chest like the beating of a Congo drum
Pleasure vibrating off my skin like sweet musk
My feet digging into the sand as if one with it
This belonging, this longing...this utter creative trouble
Manicuring itself into something I can't quite name

All these feelings I can only allow
To dwell within me as if a storm...
Seeking...the light that can only burn from within
Two candles meeting to light the world
Touching those with eyes green to brown
Have you ever been so delighted
To know that Heaven can be a key stroke away

And that hell can present itself in novelty phrases...

Where have you been that this protest for warmth has been denied?
Come dwell within the land of your mothers
Find yourself thirsty
And drink...

Douse yourself and light this match of peaceful resistance

Let hips do what lips do...lay me down here before you. swallow me up with your eyes. undress me with your hands. we only have two minutes and I insist...spread legs wide and I welcome you inside...you plunder my honey pot without breaking it. scratches up your back. a vice wrapped around you so deliciously. One final pulse and we convulse here. right here. my hair scattered against your keyboard. you lap at my apex then straighten my clothes. the door creaks open and all is as it should be..."Afternoon sir" my greeting leaves the room. 2 minutes of bliss in exchange for a claim on your soul; was the sentence worth your seed?

Eruption

Bursting within me like an A bomb
Hitting note after continuous note
Can't run from it
Can't hide from it
Leaking from these eyes like graffiti
Covered in something much more potent
What is that there called?

Tastes like sunshine and stings like rain
I felt it taking my hand when I was born
Tapping my head and encouraging me
The way the matriarch of my family does
Embracing me for the want of it all

Is that what this is?
The "want" the "will"
To allow you to breathe into existence
To drop to one knee and ask for deliverance
Begging for you to be mine

Begging for the swift turn of your pages

I feel the quaking within me
Super charged like kinetic energy
Hopelessly addicted to the next bump
Right there is where I found you
On the outskirts of the highway of disturbia
When did you make it here?
How'd I find you here...

Here pillaging books
And strangling sentences
Here punching through grammar
And caressing paragraphs
Here kissing and soothing the scars
Imitating the mission of my heart
Here dancing into sonnets
And purging into limericks

You burst within me like an A bomb
I've named you thought

There's one thing that I wear so well...makes my body sing and my
mind laugh in glee. Forms over me like a second skin; drawing the
light of day. It ignores me from the inside out. Leaving the telltale
signs of its existence as the sunsets. It awakes at 430 like
clockwork. Ringing in my bedroom like a shrill chastisement. It
dances across my sheets to tempo not all can repeat. The steps in
its gait are mesmerizing. Left untreated I feel the diagnosis would be
soul turning. There's one thing I wear so well...from the bow of my
thighs to the curve of my hips...my smile is contagious. I wear it well.

#smilemoreworryless #iammybiggestfan #mommywrites #aqueenssmile

Butterflying

My soul...hmm my soul seems to be free sometimes
It's caged in my chest like an animal
Begging for a chance...pleading for breath
And I hold it in like swimmers do
But oh how she can ignite

She burns inside me like a brush fire
Initiating the pull of hope
She fingers the curls in my hair
And forcing acceptance down my throat

I tell people my soul is black
To an extent I am right
It is scorched...
Torn apart and together by embers
Wrestling with what it means to dive
To water itself down

I only open up to and for a few
This list short and sweet like candy
Almost as sweet as she is
Blood lust she can be named

I only hold that name on my lips...
I don't speak it aloud for a name changes things
She speaks life into me
And as like flows into like
We merge together

Fire burning behind my eyes
These brown pools you get lost in
She beckons there and hopes you...
Lose yourself within me

She could devour you whole...

Change your life and mold you into something new
As she did to me...
She licks my wounds clean
From scars long since scabbed

Now I stand, back erect
Head high with flames in my eyes
She doesn't play well
But when she does...
You'll get burned

Don't you wish to be ash?

"The sun shall shine, and my heart shall sing... I've
overcome...exchange joy for my pain...I will praise..."
She woke up this morning with eyes full of forgiveness. Her heart
bursting with love. She looks in the mirror and is filled with joy. The
tears have long since dried, the bruises to her psyche have long
since healed, the scars to her mind have been honey coated and
her voice...Lord the voice you gave her shakes the souls of even the
angriest of people. She is clothed in her destiny. Where was this
woman years ago? Weeks ago? Days ago? She doesn't recognize
herself and she is excited for the shift in her demeanor. Her
footsteps light and banter contagious. Her inner smile does not falter
nor diminish. Her character is seeming to be overflowing with
happiness...what can I call her? What have you become? She
exchanged joy for her pain. No more feeling alone...her strife is all
gone. She has arrived...she will alter your life, sugar coat your hurt
and deny passage to your pain. Who am I? What have I become?
All the best and worst pieces of me and thrive on the goodness of
both. I have overcome...it must be jubilant. #holdon #nopainnomoan
#joyforyourpain #morningreflection #morningdestination
#manifestyourlife

She came baring gifts. She offered healing to your wounded,
laughter to your sad, peace to your dying and hope to your children.
She painted the night sky with stars and froze them in time to the
moon. She gave you the fruit of her bosom and the milk from her
soul. She fed the thing most important to you. She catered to your

mind. She just asked of you one thing...cherish me. The fear of this bondage scares you...you are within your right to be afraid. Her blood is filled with flames, her hair as shimmery as dew, her smile laced with arsenic and her laughter filled with fairy dust. She is everything...light and dark, good and evil, peace and war...she asks of you one thing. What would you do if she asked you?
#thebeastiscoming #mommyisapoet #pjpoetry

Apex

The buildup is killing me
It threw me against a store window
Held my arms above my head
Bit down my neck...
Like I am some savory treat...

It spread my clothed thighs...
Rubbed a hand where my warmth lies
I am there for all to see
Writhing against this glass
While you are unbothered

Flicking your fingers from the base...
Of the zipper on my jeans...that apex
Right there. Up to my lower belly
I hear the laugh stutter in your throat

God...how I need this

I purr...me purring like some animal
I'm lost; my eyes are glazed over
I can't move if you wanted me to
Frozen to this spot
Awaiting your torment

Help me I want to scream
I want to claw at you
To place your hands under...under
And you read my mind
And your hand is there...eager...

Being bathed by me
Call it blasphemous but I christened
Your pointer and middle fingers
You'll never be the same
Neither will I...

This build up is killing me
And you enjoy being named such
The lick of your tongue to my throat is my undoing

My eyes snap open...keyboard in front of me

It's been too long since my flesh tasted...
Kissed...caressed...gorged upon
Another being

I'm losing myself...Isis help me...

Split Personality

Something animalistic burns in my blood
I feel it creeping in all my extremities
I can't think over the humming in my head
I know she's going to strike

The tingle in my fingers runs down
Down my spine and rests there
In the crest of my back...
As if waiting...
Waiting to expose itself

She's awakening like a jungle cat
I stretch my body into the night
Releasing all pent up anguish
Dancing in the blood of pity
And drinking the tears of sadness

The animal in me has been asleep for years
Waiting...wanting...restless and hungry
I've slowly engaged her
Fed her appetite...11 for 2018 as requested
Her taste buds hummed in appreciation

She's begging me to blossom
To acknowledge the beast in me
Is equal to the beast in her
We cannot be bested...
My throat even sticks like glue
Trying to utter these words

She purrs out of my mouth in a sultry tone
Lead and I shall follow, she's said
Be eager and I shall leave
Be strong and sensual
The animal in you calls for it
I smile...for she speaks to me in the mirror

Pheromones attaching to the breeze
I have arrived...I shall feast

You run wild in my blood
Like something tainted and angry
Something I can't suppress
And when overwhelmed you jump out
It feels of my chest...

Or rather my mouth and I can't seem to...

Swallow you back down
This word vomit you force me to spit
These adjectives and adverbs that slowly
Waste individuals away until they are...
Simple specks I seem to find on the shirt
I left forgotten in my closet

The it's not you it's me
Is a phrase that sings true here
It stomps and hand claps like...
Gospel service on Sunday
You see...
She lives and breathes just like you
And I...

Or rather I breathe like her
Sometimes I lose the narrative of
Who's who...or what's what
She is all I am though and I am less of her
I stare in the mirror and her shadow stares back

She laughs at the tears in my eyes
Smiles at the anger in my voice
Giggles at the dismay of my heart
She is ruthless in every sense
She's plagued me into being
A puppet

She's kept me safe for so long
She's kept me sane for so long
She's kept me blind for so long
She's kept me lost for so long
She's kept me...from my potential

My emotional and irrational me
Is still a beautiful me
My spastic and comical me
Is still a beautiful me
My giddy and intellectual me
Is still a beautiful me

She's in my "me" somewhere

I'm trying to distance my "beautiful"
From her disgrace and darkness
As the tears well in my eyes again
She laughs...

Sabotage strikes again...
Dangling in front of me
Spilling like molten lava
I can't stop the spasm from hitting me
It's word vomit...

I repeat every word I've held
Expel every insecurity
Throw my anxiety to the wind
And I howl into the air

I've never felt so free
I've never been so open and accepted
The letters written on the mirror...lies
They taunt me

Echoing in my ear all the things I've always known
"You're not worth it"
"No one would want you"
"You're no one's Queen"

My hard exterior falls like glass
And all my tender pieces lay...
Bleeding on the pavement
Soaking in the coolness of the concrete

I've been in this place before
Overwhelmed with so much...
So much nothing...
It's freeing...

That after so long
Pain though I see it and I feel it
Rinse over me like a spring rain
The beating of my heart

Clarifies for me one thing

Those echoes mean nothing
Whisper to me all you'd like
Throw stones at my glass house

These shards you leave behind in your wake
Make it more dangerous for anyone else
To cross into my abyss
I can't even cry...

I feel soulless but my bridge is still strong
I will rebuild what I've made
I will wear these pieces of glass
Like a necklace

Do not enter
Do not pass
It's a dead zone

Dreamt of You

Lemme spread my legs wide
Come greet me like you should daddy
My back arching gripping your head
You licking my slit
The pressure is building
Please don't stop...

Ahhhhhh...
And you lift me to your mouth
My hips take a movement all their own
Fucking your face
My screams and mews don't stop you

The agony goes on and on
Delicious...
I crash and the tongue kissing
Doesn't stop
Until my body lays limp
Do you stop...I shiver...

Spreading my legs

I welcome you in
You hover over me
Face a mix of emotions...
The tip pushes in
A smile breaks my lips

Your breath hitches
Inch by inch you encase yourself
My legs wrap your waist
Bringing your pelvis to mine

Fuck me like you own every cell
That exists in me...
This is yours...

Let our story start again

The Ride

You have no idea how my name on your lips...
Feels to me...
When you utter the simple syllables
My body is transferred elsewhere
My mind picks up things my face doesn't...
Give away...

A name...so simple as it rolls off the tongue
You say my name as if...

As if it's a bittersweet wine
That you enjoy in the back of your throat
That you swish around to taste over and over

While in this tasting...I feel so many other things
My mind's eye is fogged with digital images of you
Sinful images...

My arms pinned behind my back
On my knees
Chest to the bed
Head turned to the side
My hair wild like a crown at my head

Your one hand clasped around both my wrists
One hand at my hips
Your legs encased mine
Your dick rubbing my lips
My mouth moaning "fuck me"

And so...you do...

You caress me in ways only you can
You take me to the edge and pull me back
With each stroke I'm reaching the pentacle
The cliff is so close and you move me from it
"Not yet" you utter in my ear as your chest
Touches my back

I am already lost to everything
My mind only knows touch
Words I can't form
And there you are...
Pushing and branding me

And you've found the spot
It's right there...I feel the smile on your lips
My hips quiver, my breathing intensifies
My hands grip the sheets shredding them
But you don't stop
Then your hand moves from my hip to my clit

Blue light crushes into my vision
And I'm lost...screaming out so loud
I'm breathless
You're not finished with me yet...

"We have all night"
You whisper into the night
And pull me atop you
"Round 2 begins"

And I begin my ride...

Invisible Touch

Why won't you let me touch you...
I know you can feel my mind...
Summoning you
Calling out to you

More like screaming out to you
Breathlessly...

But for now I greet you on the stage
Sitting with a microphone to my lips
Wishing that you would strip me
Here...
For all to see

Because you are the audience
An audience of one
Listening to my vocals strum
Into the silence of this room

It's darker then I imagined
The light right above me
But your smile is still the same
Still slow to appear

If I stroke down my throat

Down lower still...
Squeeze my breast
Is that appropriate here?
On this stage?

Lower still...
Watching you watch me
The lights dimming on me
Clutching both the mic
And my...

Can't you come here and fill me
Feel me...guide me onto
The girth of you
So my falsetto can ring into...
The night?

Your name is sugar on my tongue
Sweet...a craving of mine
Let me nibble your lips...
Let me ride you here
Here and now

Just take the first step...

Join the show

Hunting You

Honey you look like you're ready
Ready for me to rip your life apart
You look hungry for it even
Even a little bit eager

I see you watching my lips move
Watching how close my mouth gets...
To this microphone I'm caressing
And I see your eyes glued to my words
Or rather my face

Do you imagine what my mouth can do...

Do to yours...
And other ungodly things...
Cause Heaven knows there's so many...
To name...

Like how my tongue can curl up and around
The tip of your...

But as I said it's something you're hungry for
Your hands are sweating
Breath heavy
You watch me fondle the base...
Of my throat
And I can see your mind racing

I can even hear your heart pounding
Like a drum...
The same way you want to encase me
Pounding away as I scream into ecstasy
Your name on my lips

You're waiting I can see
You're just out of reach
First row, third table
Wiping your palms on your denim jeans
I'm already wet I'm sure you're aware
Dripping the sweetest of dew

All of this beauty poured into a maroon dress
Do you wish to see me out of it
Wish for me to allow you in
To fill these walls with something akin to...
New life...to refresh your soul

Allow me to feed you
I warned you...I'll rip your life apart
Oh but the falling of it feels so good
Don't walk away hungry...

Come...

Slowly

Cool against your cheeks
Feather weight in your hands
Sliding so gently down
You wouldn't have known it was there

Disappearing like a lovers smile
Welcomed and unwelcome like a ghost
It plays against your face
Dancing to a beat of a drum

Slowly and ever so silent
Your voice in your throat
The down of your comforter
A reminder...

A reminder of the scent you can't forget
A reminder of the warmth you can't forget
How an arm rested around you
A tight embrace
A reminder of a heart beat
A warm body...breath

A reminder of love...

His boots still scatter the floor
His alarm still blaring like a trumpet
His keys on the nightstand
The empty bed is your only knowledge
The only thing you wish wasn't true

His dog tags hang around your neck
His picture across the room
His smile on his face
His laughter in his eyes

He's not coming home...you know this
And the tears start again
The war may have buried him
But he will live forever in your heart

Allow the feather weight of the tears to fall

A reminder of the love you still know
Hold your blanket a little tighter
A piece of him you will always have...

His daughter will come soon
You rub your belly with a sad smile
His laughter she is sure to have
But for now it's okay...

To lay there and cry.

Plausible

The most vulnerable I have ever been is with you
You have been the one that picks the pieces back up
Whether you see the splitting of my soul or not
You didn't make me feel like a monster
You didn't make me feel unworthy
Never when speaking to you have I been afraid to be me

Learning the difference between love and like is passion
This passion scares me...
Everyone runs...and I'm left filling
Myself back up...
I've loved myself for a while
But never have I been more afraid...
More sub conscious about my words
In hopes that my passion doesn't fall deafly

Have you ever looked love in the face and ran?

You've allotted me the chance to feel and be free...
All I want is you to float in the freeness of it with me...

If that's what they call a cross between passion and love
Set sail with me...

Ballooning

I'm floating away
So cold into the distant night
Taken away with the wisp of your hair
Dangling on strands hung on your wrist
I can't breathe without you
I can't live without you

I am tied around you snuggly
Why don't you caress me anymore
Why don't you blow me those kisses again
You used to dance with me
You used to hold me close

Now I can't breathe
Now I can't move

The wind picks me up
You decided to leave me here
I'm not the one you want to take home

I move across the floor
Swaying to an invisible beat
Praying you come back
The lights go down
The music dies
But you don't see me here

I'm in the corner watching kiss you her
I realized you're not taking me home
I'll keep dancing on my own
Until the lights come up
Look this way, see me again
I gave you my all
It's a shame...

I deflate
And continue to dance on my own

Savage

I've wanted to claim your soul
Not just your body

Though how delicious it will be
To mold my body to yours
To take the essence of you
Empty all of you into me
And then I will take of you
Claim your soul and intertwine it...
With mine...
Stroke your mental state
Until my lips and my hands
Massage you into delirium
I want to lay claim to you as a man
Until your mind is a fog of me
Til my voice soothes you
Like a balm
I would fear it
I would fear me if I was you...
I've been hunting you for a while...

Fairytales

Your skin glistens in the pale moon light
You're bathed in the most delightful setting
You have obliged me by removing all...
Incumbrances...stripped bare before me
A sheet is entangled around your legs

My mouth waters looking at you
My tongue aches for your taste
My skin hums in recognition of you
Delicious...

I wrap my lips around the tip of you
The salty sweetness tingling my throat
My fingers milk you
My smile spreads as you lift me down to you

My legs encase you like a vice
The ride has begun with quick
Steady movements
Moonlight kisses our skin

We are the picture of perfection
I ride into the sunrise
Your name on my lips

What a glorious wet dream

Who?

If I empty myself who will I be

If I disappear into these clouds

Control-less

Wrap your arms around me

Capture me in your vice grip

My feet are butterfly kisses to the pavement

I know this isn't love

I know that this is wrong

But just hold me a little longer

This is all I need right now

Just for this moment

Stay with me

I heard you whisper my name
I heard your raspy undertones
I heard your gasp of glee
I heard you dissect my name

In what dimension was it palpable
To breathe my name into that empty space
Why utter syllables you cannot understand

I will mourn your life

Did you not know better
Did you not believe I would come for you
While you try to spread deceit

Why bring your lips to form a name
Who's power you don't understand
Why evoke something in me
Why call upon if you are not ready for...

Your end...

I pray that your mental death is swift
And your cowardly walk is eternal
After today you will know who I am

The Great Devourer

The sound of metal against glass
Can you hear it?
The sound of nails against a chalk board
Can you hear if?
The sound of a tree falling in the woods
Can you hear it?

Her footsteps are as silent
As an empty forest
And as deadly as a heat wave
Plague she is not, but promise she can be

She promises to possess you
In a way no other woman chooses to
She allotted you time in her Haven
She gave you drinks of her soul

The only thing she requires
Is a blood offering
Bring her your wife
Bring her your life
Bring her your ups
Your downs
Most importantly
Bring her your knowledge

Pledge yourself only to her
And she may spare you
She may awaken your cerebral
And leave you wanting

She is sin and forgiveness
She is Africa
Embrace her

9 798631 520738